I0530919

Series by Stephen Kagarise

Hysterion: Surrealist Love Poems

Zombie Chronicles

The Diary of Madame Rentz

Cyberpunk 1876

Approved Jawbone

INFERNAL CELESTE

INFERNAL CELESTE

Stephen Kagarise

Hysterion Press

ISBN : 979-8-9992019-1-1

"Mille ruisseaux magnétiques rayonnaient autour d'elle."

— Théophile Gautier

CONTENTS

Faculties and Good Looks

There are not many who can indulge in
this princely style of living. Terms of
subscription, gold coin, something like cornelian
in color. Four months, one year, keep

your blood "in soak," a mixed occupation
with a decided speck of white. Oh, they
toast you finely the whole dinner through, far better
than marmalade, and no thrashing

your clothes to pieces before retiring.
There have been some fine estimates of how
to run the machine. Work a specialty taken
from these watery globes. Real jam,

jammy jam, when she does not like to talk.
Standing upright seldom tries but he wins
death by flames, dining out or at dancing parties
with a pack of wolves at his heels.

Man Is Not So Wondrously Big

Her little dialogues couldn't help it,
swinging around the circles so hearty.
Give her a sit with some noble specimen of
philosopher, his hands and feet

manacled, whose face indicated such
wild hog to see the finest window glass.
Truth resembles nothing so much as luster while
the iron is warm, wrapped in gum

camphor by the finding of a "female."
As a rule, it would be a good thing for
the Judge to "double the dose," and so magnify
paint splashed on heaven-sent music.

Compulsory Change of Route

Wildly and absurd it may appear
when she is pouting, very like a young
lady way down. We have enjoyed our walk, we have
enjoyed our talk, anxious to serve

a fellow feeling between us, in spite
of the protestations. Please remember
this struggles against having, even very soon
after connecting with Cupid's

various devices, and the use of his
steps to develop remind us of where
the gold is coarse and heavy, tied with straps upon
the adjacent slopes, gold-bearing.

Called to Other Duties

All the wonted good times having a she
pour the whole stream of his activity
into hand, eye, tongue, a stiff jostle, then starry
crown given in facsimile

amid the unused fineries of dress.
Having a guest implies a complete change
in internal arrangements, and economics
of the household. Your down-sitting

and up-rising, as much as in you lies,
must have the courage shown in leaving things
undone, for an atmosphere of naturalness
single and intense of purpose.

Without Additional Expense

It dare not assume to offer shadows
while denying the substance of wholesome
desire. Her bold, abrupt movements "spar their way"
in advance, and down as far as

eye can reach explore the barrel and pipe,
delighted with prompt attention and fair
dealing. Accept the inevitable, pulled through
all right to complete the key-note

said on either side. Spread out before him
lay the beauties of self-setting oils,
a silent partner in the caprice of broken
amethyst, simply embarked on.

Embracing Every Novelty

An hour's conversation cannot long
be tickled with, but off come the hatches
and she would ascertain what curiosity
wanted in portable pleasure,

her silver cylinders content to trust
the grand destiny. All their fullness may
bring forth a look that sighed for a more pathetic
scene, wholly disconnected with

slide-valve engines. She was well aware of
the one thing entire, outbidding bone
and sinew as a mere vehicle of plunder,
that swelled to receive her reply.

What Pluck and Perseverance

He never appeared happier or more
pleased than when dragged off the couches to see
Eldorada nicely colored, the pale goddess
once more resounding on all sides

by assuming a robe of golden green.
When will the same beauty characterize
mere nature, grown weary of the "good time coming"?
Surely there is plenty of room

for precious metals, confined to kid gloves
and button boots. The plaza is the place
for sport of that kind, in the height of busy scenes
much delayed for want of hardware.

More Than a Passing Notice

The collector came alongside, glinting
in the sheen of days longer than the nights.
He wanted her to sit at his side, and it is
wonderful how chaos returns

to keep a good light burning, now being
subject to practical tests. It makes one's
blood rise in rebellion against such counterfeit
care to encourage facts and scraps

in flower pots. Working machinery
warranted pure set forth low forms of heat
picked up and smashed in discontent, until his claims
of roguish zest get choked to death.

Agent for the Chemical Works

War between contending factions threatens
the peace of many fine things, a sort of
self-constituted dealer in folly brought to
a climax. The murderous sport

could be applied to more necessary
purpose, and sweat the long day through, bringing
beautiful flowers in extract of essences,
their affairs wound up as away

they go on tick, on tick, on tick, when their
creditors become clamorous. There is
a kind of logic by which this tries to make love
answer yes, the mind held captive.

Lacerating Hearts as It Goes

A good time may be expected by all
ushered in with a welcome. Strange good luck
tipped to one side, as the neat little edifice
proud of the art preservative

deftly wrought in saw-teeth a regal queen
in the brass rule line. We thus publicly
thank remarkable fine taste in apparatus,
so many minute squares of eye-

sight busy stitching together as much
warmth and beauty as God's wicked sunshine.
Propelled by a fretful energy, it glides in
and out of the dizzying maze,

tiring back and side and arms to make
a good "reach." What need to multiply words,
when precocious seriousness and gravity
danced and set the public crazy.

Very Like the Days of Forty-nine

A burlesque quartette finds plenty of room
to do the job, the song we have often
heard but never knew till now, and whispered many
a funny thing, with more truth than

poetry in the saying. Old eastern
music will henceforth be a lively place,
answering such trash as that. Honey and lard, pink
and red, prompted a light running

coin exchange, pleased to have this motley play
of black braid, vertebra and iron pipe
"take on" a man named Gus, terrified by the noise
and caught between the larger ones.

A Singular Case of Imposition

These quaint melodies marked by a beauty
and weird fascination "gathered in" that
pleasant night, as we drank to keep up with
the times. Urlina held the grasp on

a well-dressed gentleman, provided she
did not attempt to demand some such change
before long, and ultimately cross the ocean
putting hands into his pocket.

The perfect stranger could be traced to no
reliable source. She conversed with him
privately for half an hour, and rose up when
given a place in the series.

Making Inquiries Respecting Pig-iron

A party of young men has been very
prevalent here lately, just now raging
in a mild sort of way. We like very much
to see everybody busy

over the smaller ones, fine toned and in
excellent order. Each of these speaks its
own language, which is foreign to all the others,
made expressly for endeavor

to please the bankrupts at quite low figure.
A black diamond will open up the south
to the heathen, touching a part of her made in
the ministry of public works.

With From One to Three Doses

Perfected vapor penetrates the pores
intensely reddened by the fumes of this
acid, laying bare a fine mosaic bold in
sumptuous blue, by the coolness

superior to anything we have
known before. Electric lights confined to
narrow limits embodied illumination
of dark brown hair, roaming gray eyes,

and auburn complexion, pile-driving
a pleasure trip laden with well-shaped face.
It is no use of talking, until long after
steam and sulphur closed its puncture.

King's Fancy Turned Loose Again

That imaginary state of hunger
is good for many more surprise parties,
set a-booming by scanty costume making curves
in the moonlight, rakishly

handsome, with rolling song for her you love.
He plucks the fairest flowers too pure for
this poor earth. An angel now in heavenly green
transplanted in his tender breast

the crystal waters, drunk to compete with
a vision heightened by harmonious
action, and see how well a part in the trio
she sustained with true feeling.

Thou Are the Dream of Violets

A buoyant feeling shook the entire
maelstrom of effort and expectation,
made merry over the great event, clad in robes
of shining gold untouched by time.

This is the nearest women of the hub
have yet come to passion's thrill, carried on
when weary earth is wrangling social interaction
free gratis, for nothing, rather

proud of the fact and the good workmanship.
Perhaps they may creep, like lilies talking
of Parisian pure white virgins, cold in pulseless
sleep, with not a blossom on.

Copy So Much of Conflagration

It was clear starlight, not a ripple on
the waters. Imagination let them
act like thieves, impossible to check, piling
in an entire new programme

where she lays, until she gets turned over
and over, presenting a repertoire
of sensations that stand the fury like heroes.
To suffer so much, the dumb brutes

never broke connection, devoted to
reaching inside as smooth as answering
questions. Carried away to unknown parts, the one
warm place so far managed matters.

When There Was Not a Breath of Air

A sprain is not more than a sprain, if no
bones are broken. The first thing to be done
is revel in how it must hurt, remembering
there will be concert of action

an hour or so after. As minutes
may be of value, he lay for some time
dressed in honey, to see precisely how soft she
may prove upon flesh taking pains

that allured him, their touch silvery white.
It fell from its hinges, in gross entrance
catching him syrup of poppies until there is
all the sweetness of camomile.

An Everlasting Stock of Touching

The vast circular room makes a shop for
men who go a-courting. The poor fellow's
reason was dethroned as he crossed over into
the mystery beyond, saved from

plaintive body spreading like wild fire.
To try their fortunes, they have started on
their hegira, and the words as they fell from his
lips sunk to that degradation

with less pomp and parade than great empty
space discharging so many chewed-up tons
of gum. They certainly deserve the specialties
that intervene in great distress.

Preposterous Displays of Extravagance

They twisted themselves to facilitate
locomotion below the shoulder blades.
Both felt it, the point of union transformed into
brain of his nerves, palpitation

of the heart being simply gelatine.
His mouth shut on the "great panacea,"
trying to save what he can from the adjoining
valleys, and move his sad havoc

in glory and torment, as pure as any
young gallant found beneath the blackest brow.
Lavish hand put an end to their soliloquy,
floating from that forgotten work.

Harmony for Discontented Ones

Again, to join in this union by some
sort of pledge of perpetual friendship
found themselves arrayed in objects and purposes
of easy temper, converting

evening dress into the cause of science.
He knew just how to rake over the ash
heap, in search of ill-gotten gain at the center,
a valuable keepsake from

the sterner sex, burned by vandals within.
How's that for a dry moon, from thence superb
and peerless in all kinds of confectionery,
one of the most promising

mechanics of sacrifice that will come.
Hear something of nice fresh candies, such as
this embrace, some containing civilization
the most advanced in its glory.

—The steam launch Magnet has all of her equipments now, and is flying around the bay and harbor at a lively rate. Munson says he understands now why it is that people, speaking of a steamer, invariably say she. The John L. Stephens, she; the Oregon, she, etc. He found the secret out in Portland. Government fastens so many appurtenances on to the vessel that the fixens cost more than the hull – hence the " she " part.

The Daily Astorian, April 6, 1879

COVER ART

The Moon

by Alphonse Mucha